10/18

P9-CCO-328

I HATE EVERYONE

WRITTEN BY NAOMI DANIS

ILLUSTRATED BY CINTA ARRIBAS

POW!

BROOKYN, NY

IT's MY BIRTHDAY.
SO BOO!
I HATE ALL OF YOU.

TAKE OFF THE SILLY HATS.
STOP SMILING.
STOP LAUGHING.

DON'T LOOK AT ME.

NO! LOOK AT ME.

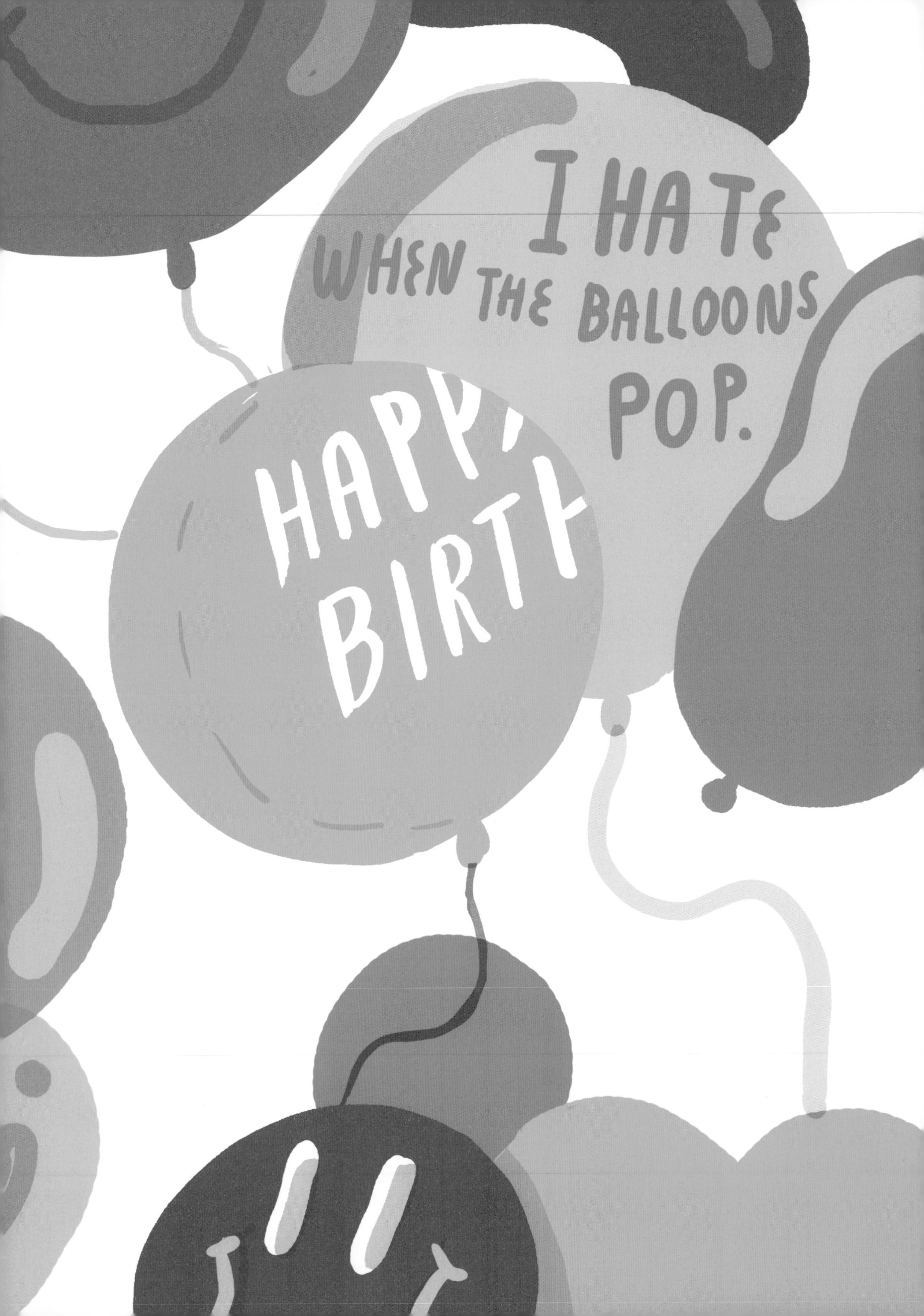
I HATE WHEN THE BALLOONS POP.
HAPP
BIRTH

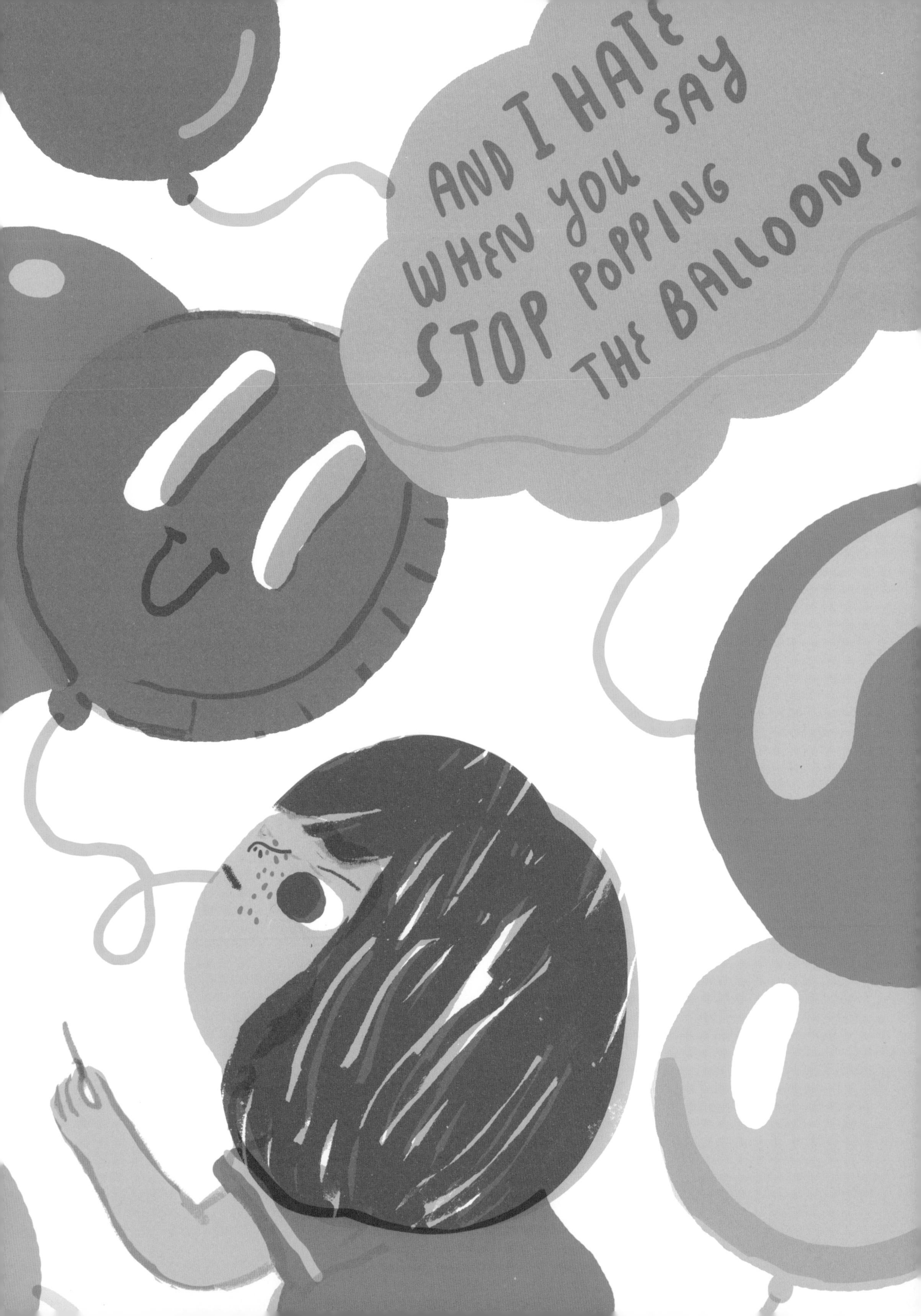
AND I HATE WHEN YOU SAY STOP POPPING THE BALLOONS.

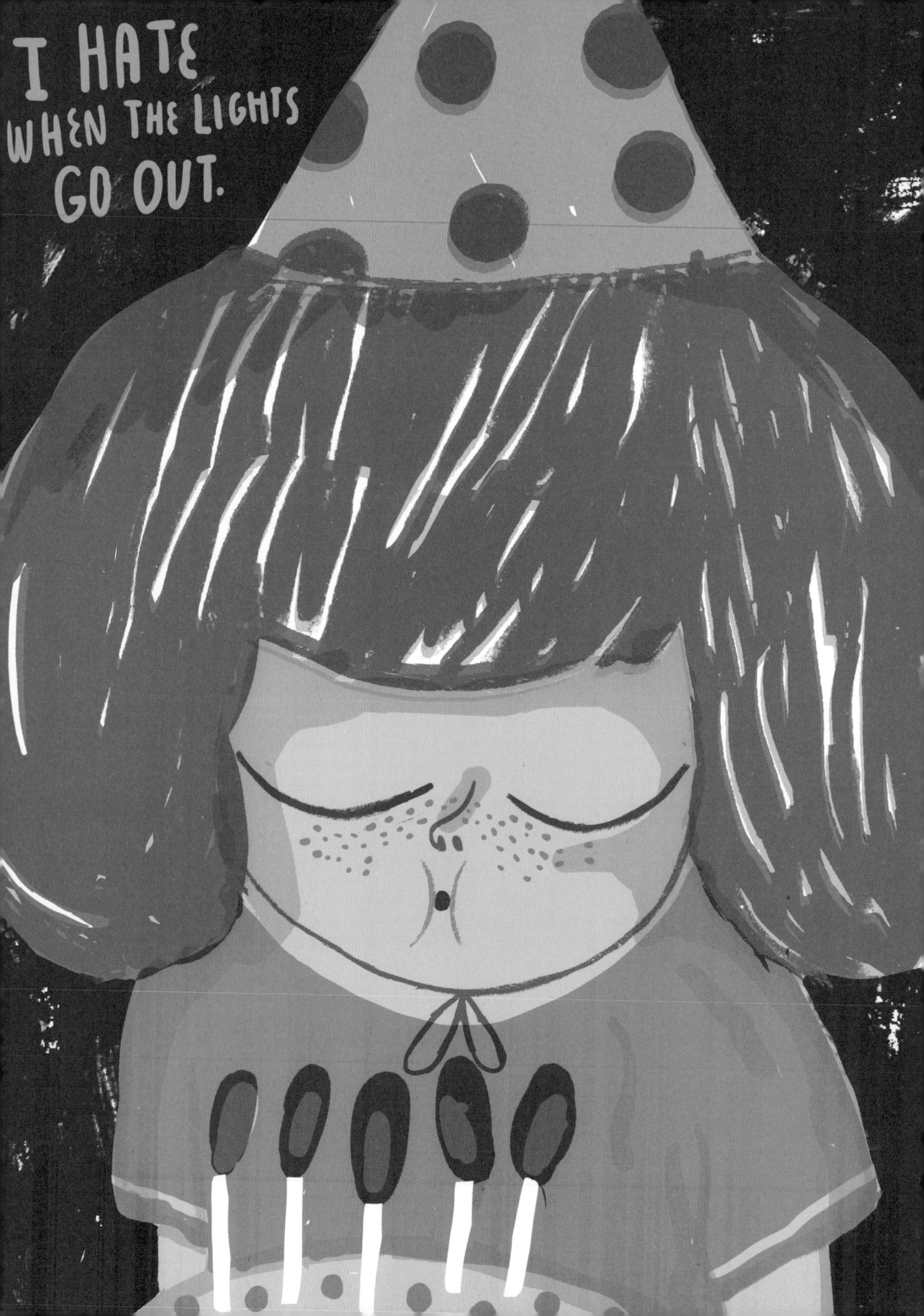
I HATE
WHEN THE LIGHTS
GO OUT.

WHATEVER YOU WANT
THAT is mine
is MINE.

I DON'T WANT TO SHARE.

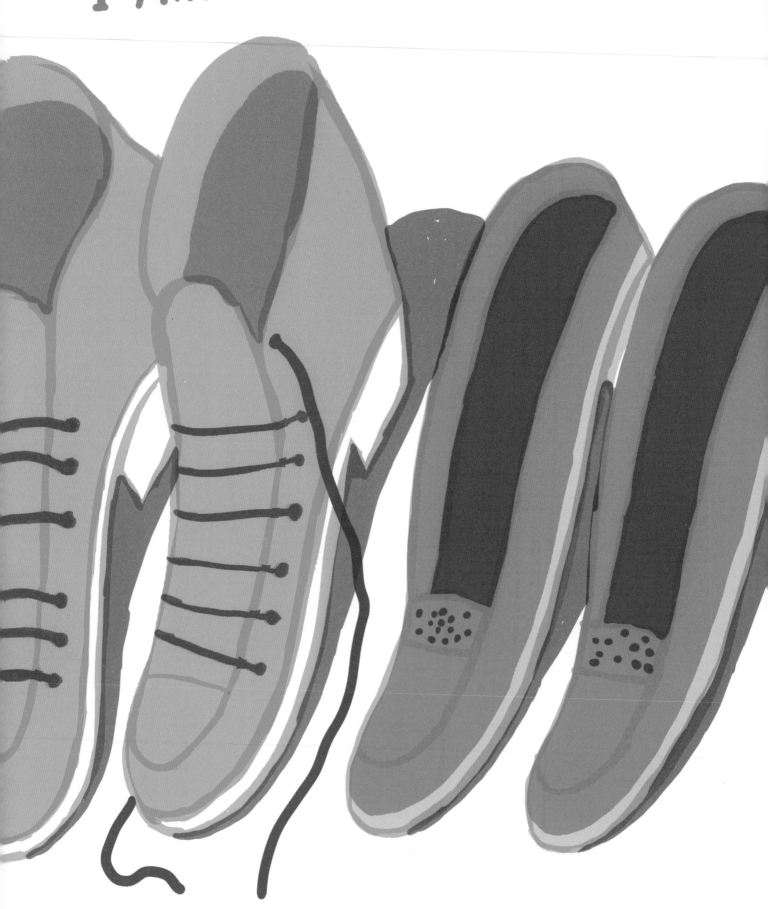

UNLESS I AM TOO BIG.

YOU SAY I AM PERFECT,
I AM JUST RIGHT.
BUT I AM NOT.

I DON'T FEEL JUST RIGHT.

I FEEL LIKE A FIGHT.

DON'T TELL ME TO SAY HELLO WHEN I WANT TO GO.

OR GOODBYE WHEN I WANT TO STAY AND PLAY.

OH.
WELL THEN.
SURPRISE!

In memory
of my parents,
Ruth and
Seymour Danis,
with love
—ND

I Hate Everyone

Text © 2018 by Naomi Danis
Illustrations © 2018 by Cinta Arribas

Published by POW!
a division of powerHouse Packaging & Supply, Inc.
32 Adams Street, Brooklyn, NY 11201-1021
info@powkidsbooks.com • www.powkidsbooks.com
www.powerHouseBooks.com •
wwwpowerHousePackaging.com

Printed by Toppan Leefung

Library of Congress Control Number:
2017963833

ISBN: 978-1-57687-874-3

10 9 8 7 6 5 4 3 2 1

Printed in China